W9-AEX-842

SycamoreStreet

by C. B. Christiansen
illustrations by Melissa Sweet

Atheneum   1993   New York

Maxwell Macmillan Canada
Toronto

Maxwell Macmillan International
New York   Oxford   Singapore   Sydney

Atheneum
Macmillan Publishing Company
866 Third Avenue
New York, NY 10022

Maxwell Macmillan Canada, Inc.
1200 Eglinton Avenue East
Suite 200
Don Mills, Ontario M3C 3N1

Macmillan Publishing Company is part of
the Maxwell Communication Group of Companies.

First edition

Printed in Hong Kong by South China Printing Company (1988) Ltd.
10 9 8 7 6 5 4 3 2 1
The text of this book is set in 14 pt. Baskerville.
The illustrations are rendered in watercolor.
Library of Congress Cataloging-in-Publication Data
Christiansen, C. B.
    Sycamore Street / by C. B. Christiansen; illustrations by Melissa Sweet. — 1st ed.
        p.   cm.
    Summary: Best friends Angel and Chloe spend the passing seasons enjoying
the outdoors and trying to avoid the obnoxious Rupert Raguso—until Angel
goes away for two weeks and Chloe needs someone to play with.
    ISBN 0-689-31784-0
    [1. Friendship—Fiction.   2. Seasons—Fiction.]   I. Sweet, Melissa,
ill.   II. Title.
PZ7.C45285Sy   1993
[E]—dc20   92-33685

For my sister, Mary Kay,
a forever friend
—C.B.C.

In memory of John R. Mader
—M.S.

Contents

Angel and Chloe ate the cherries and spit the pits.

Pooh!

One pit landed in the grass.

Pooh! Pooh!

Two pits landed on the curb.

Pooh! Pooh! Pooh!

Three pits landed in the street.

"Chloe," said Angel, "you are the best pit-spitter on Sycamore Street."

"Yours went farther," said Chloe. "You are the Princess of Pits."

Angel giggled and touched her crown. "The Princess of Pits," she said. "I like that."

Chloe spit another pit. It landed on the sidewalk by someone's foot.

"The cherries are ripe," said Angel.

"Let's pick some," said Chloe.

"Sure," said Angel. "I love cherries."

"We live on the best street in the world," said Chloe.

Angel sighed. "If it weren't for Rupert Raguso, life would be perfect on Sycamore Street."

Angel and Chloe climbed their tree.

"Let's pretend," said Chloe.

"Yes, let's pretend," said Angel. "But what should we pretend?"

"Princesses," said Chloe.

Chloe made a cherry-leaf crown and put it on her head.

Angel made a cherry-leaf crown and put it on her head.

They looked out over their kingdom.

"Watch out for Rupert," said Angel.

"Poor old Rupert," said Chloe. "He doesn't know how to pretend."

"He can't even pretend to be nice," said Angel.

Chloe picked a handful of cherries. "Now that we are princesses, we can have a royal feast."

Angel picked a handful of cherries. "*Mmm, a feast of royal fruit.*"

1

Pretending

Angel and Chloe tiptoed down Sycamore Street.

Chloe looked to the right.

Angel looked to the left. "Do you see Rupert-the-Moose-o-Raguso?" she asked.

"No," said Chloe. "We're in luck."

Rupert, the new boy, was nowhere in sight.

Angel and Chloe walked past the old sycamore tree. It stood by itself at the end of the block. They came to a row of cherry trees and stopped at the biggest one.

"Who could that be?" asked Chloe.

Angel looked through the branches. "Oh no," she said, "it's Rupert Raguso. What do we do now?"

Chloe put her finger to her lips. "Let's pretend," she whispered.

"Let's pretend what?" whispered Angel.

"Let's pretend we are invisible," said Chloe.

5

Rupert climbed the tree next to Angel and
Chloe's tree. He waved.

"Don't wave to us," said Angel.

"Why not?" asked Rupert.

Angel sighed. "Can't you see we are
invisible?"

Rupert shook his head and frowned.

"I think you made him sad," said Chloe.
"After all, Rupert doesn't know about
pretending."

Rupert made a cherry-leaf crown and put it
on his head.

Angel rolled her eyes. "That's a funny-
looking crown. It doesn't even fit."

Rupert turned red in the face.

"Uh-oh," said Chloe. "Now you've made him mad."

Rupert ate some cherries. Rupert spit some pits. Rupert aimed the pits at Angel and Chloe.

Pooh!

One pit whizzed past Chloe's ear.

Pooh! Pooh!

Two pits bounced off Angel's arm.

Pooh! Pooh! Pooh!

Three pits landed in her cherry-leaf crown.

"Ick!" said Chloe.

"Ouch!" said Angel. "That is no way to treat the Princess of Pits."

Angel and Chloe climbed down from their tree.

"Rupert ruins everything," said Angel. "He'll never know how to pretend."

"*We* can still pretend," said Chloe.

Angel twirled her cherry-leaf crown. "What should we pretend?"

Pooh! Pooh! Pooh! Pooh! Pooh!

Five cherry pits rained down from Rupert's tree.

Angel ducked and ran.

Chloe ducked and ran after her.

"*I* know," said Chloe. "We can pretend Rupert doesn't live on Sycamore Street."

2

Magic

The leaves fell off the sycamore tree. The branches were bare by Halloween.

Angel and Chloe dressed up as witches.

"I'm flying," said Chloe.

Angel ran. "So am I! So am I!" Her black cape billowed behind her.

Little trick-or-treaters turned around to watch.

Chloe cackled.

Angel screeched.

They snickered in their most wicked way.

The little trick-or-treaters clapped their hands.

"We're not scaring *anyone*," said Angel. "We didn't scare the scarecrow. We didn't scare the cat. We didn't scare the hobo. We didn't scare the bat."

"I have an idea," said Chloe. "Let's make them disappear."

"Disappear," said Angel. "Good idea! *Alakabam-Kazoo!*" she shouted.

Angel and Chloe twirled around three times. *"Alakabam-Kazoo!"* they shouted together.

They stopped twirling.

There stood the scarecrow. There stood the cat. There stood the hobo. There stood the bat.

"Boo!" said Angel.

"Boo!" said Chloe.

"Boo!" said the little trick-or-treaters.

Angel and Chloe didn't scare anyone. Not even Rupert-the-Greedy-Raguso, who had two costumes and went to each house twice.

Rupert-the-Frankenstein followed them up one side of Sycamore Street.

"We know it's you, Rupert," said Chloe.

Rupert-the-Frankenstein rolled his eyes and moaned.

Angel grabbed Chloe's arm and held on tight. "You don't scare us," she said.

Rupert-the-Werewolf followed them down the other side of Sycamore Street.

"We know it's you, Rupert," said Chloe.

Rupert-the-Werewolf howled. "Ahrooooo!"

Angel and Chloe walked a little faster.

"Who's afraid of a werewolf?" asked Chloe.

"Not me," said Angel. She called over her shoulder, "You shouldn't try to scare people, Rupert. It isn't nice."

"I have an idea," said Chloe. "Let's make Rupert disappear."

"Good idea," said Angel. *"Alakabam-Kazoo!"*

Angel and Chloe squeezed their eyes shut. *"Alakabam-Kazoo!"* they shouted together.

They opened their eyes.

There stood Rupert with two full bags. "Trick or treat," he said from behind his mask. "Want some of my candy?"

"Really?" asked Chloe. She held out her hand.

"No! It's a trick!" said Angel. "Come *on.*"
Angel and Chloe hurried from door to door,
but Rupert stayed close behind them.
They came to the end of Sycamore Street.
It was time to go home.
Angel and Chloe waved their broomsticks.
"Good night, Scarecrow."

"Good night, Cat."
"Good night, Hobo."
"Good night, Bat."
"Good night, Rupert-the-Greedy-
Frankenstein-Werewolf-Raguso."
"We know it's you," said Angel.
"It is *not* me," said Rupert.

17

When Angel and Chloe got to Chloe's house, they took off their witch hats and took off their witch capes and emptied their bags on the living room floor.

Chloe picked up a chocolate bar.

Angel picked up a handful of caramels.

"I have an idea," said Chloe. "Let's make this candy disappear."

"Good idea," said Angel.

"Alakabam-Kazoo!"

And they did.

3

Figure-Eight Friends

The pond by Angel's house was frozen.

Angel and Chloe bundled up in their matching red scarves and matching blue mittens. They laced up their matching white skates.

They teetered and tottered as they circled the ice.

Chloe lifted her arms over her head. "I'm spinning," she sang.

Angel giggled puffs of air. "I'm spinning, too!"

"I'm getting dizzy," said Chloe.

"So am I," said Angel. "Who is that skating on our pond?"

19

Chloe stopped spinning and rubbed her eyes. "It's Rupert Raguso," she said, "and he's getting closer."

Rupert skidded by.

"He's not really skating," said Angel. "He's just sliding on his shoes."

Rupert lifted his arms over his head.

"I think he wants to skate with us," said Chloe.

"No, he's making fun of us," said Angel.

"I don't care," said Chloe. "We're having a good time and we are friends."

Angel smiled. "We are figure-eight friends forever."

"Yes," said Chloe, "forever and ever."

Angel and Chloe skated to the edge.

Rupert skidded by backward.

"Rupert will do anything for attention," said Angel.

Angel and Chloe peeled off their matching blue mittens to unlace their matching white skates.

Rupert skidded by with one leg in the air.

"He's pretty good," said Chloe.

"He's just showing off," said Angel.

"Brrr," said Chloe. "My fingers are cold." She reached for her mittens.

"I'm sorry," said Angel, "but those are mine."

"Oh, no," said Chloe, "I think they are mine."

"They're not!" said Angel. She grabbed the mittens.

"That's no way to treat a forever friend,"

said Chloe. She folded her arms across her
chest. "If those are yours, then where are
mine?"

Rupert skidded by backward with one leg
in the air and a blue mitten thumb sticking out
of his pocket.

Angel and Chloe looked at each other.

"How did he do that?" asked Chloe.

Angel shrugged. "He's just Rupert-the-Sneaky-Raguso, I guess."

"Sneaking off with *my* blue mittens," said Chloe.

She rubbed her fingers together. "It's too cold to fight with each other *or* Rupert. *I* know. Let's pretend."

"Okay," said Angel. "Let's pretend what?"

Chloe thought for a moment. "Let's pretend we *each* lost a mitten."

Angel and Chloe left the frozen pond with their matching white skates and matching red scarves, sharing a pair of matching blue mittens.

"Figure-eight friends forever," said Chloe.

"Figure-eight friends forever," said Angel.

They held their matching bare hands all the way down Sycamore Street.

4

Poor Chloe

Spring rain fell through the sycamore tree.

Chloe walked to Angel's house. Her yellow boots went *clump, clump* on the sidewalk.

Chloe jumped in a big puddle and made a big splash.

She jumped in a bigger puddle and made a bigger splash.

She jumped in the biggest puddle on Sycamore Street and sank to the top of her buckles.

Chloe liked walking in the rain in her bright yellow boots.

When she got to Angel's house, she
stomped her boots on the porch.

The door opened.

"Poor Chloe! You are soaked!" said Angel's
mother. "Come right in. You, too, Rupert.
Don't be shy."

Chloe turned around.

There stood Rupert-the-Soggy-Raguso.
Raindrops bounced off the bill of his cap.

"You're just in time for cocoa," said
Angel's mother.

Angel sat at the kitchen table, looking at a
postcard of a sunny beach with a blue sky.

Angel smiled at Chloe.

Angel frowned at Rupert.

Angel's mother set three mugs of cocoa on

the table. "Marshmallows?" she asked.

"I'll have one, please," said Chloe.

"One, please," said Angel.

Rupert held up five fingers. "Please,"
he said.

Angel's mother crowded the marshmallows into Rupert's mug.

Angel and Chloe looked at each other.

Angel sniffed and snorted like a pig.

Chloe sniffed and snorted like a pig.

"Do you girls need tissues?" asked Angel's mother.

Then it was Rupert's turn to snort.

Angel showed Chloe the postcard.

"We're going to a warm, sunny beach," she said. "We'll be gone for two whole weeks!"

Rupert-the-Piggy-Raguso slurped up two of his five fat marshmallows.

Chloe's marshmallow felt stuck in her throat. It was hard to imagine two whole weeks without Angel.

"I'll send you a postcard, Chloe," said Angel.

"And Rupert, too," said Angel's mother.

Angel sighed. "And Rupert, too."

"Is it fun at the beach?" Chloe asked.

"Sure," said Angel. "We'll swim in the ocean. We'll play in the sand. The sun will shine every day. Best of all, it *won't rain*."

Chloe looked out the kitchen window.

Rain fell. The sky was gray.

"I like rain," said Rupert.

Me, too, thought Chloe.

"Poor Chloe," said Angel. "I wish you were coming with us."

"And Rupert, too," said Angel's mother.

Angel sighed. "And Rupert, too."

"I'll miss you, Angel," said Chloe.

Rupert didn't say anything. His mouth was full of marshmallow.

On the way home from Angel's house, Chloe's boots went *clump, clump* on the sidewalk. She tilted her head back and caught a raindrop on her tongue.

Chloe jumped and splashed in all the puddles on Sycamore Street.

She thought about Angel swimming in the ocean and playing in the sand and being in a place where the sun shone every day.

No sidewalks.

No puddles.

No *clump, clump,* jump, splash!

Chloe walked past the old sycamore tree. It stood by itself at the end of the block.

Two weeks without a friend, thought Chloe. Poor Angel. I wish she could stay home with me and walk in the rain in her bright yellow boots.

5

Monkeys

There was no one to play with on Sycamore Street. Angel was away on her trip. When the cherry trees bloomed, the petals fell.

They fell on the ground.

They fell on Chloe.

They fell on Rupert-the-Shadow-Raguso.

Chloe missed Angel and she missed pretending. She carried Angel's postcard in her pocket. Two weeks was a long time to be without a friend.

Chloe watched the petals fall. "If Angel were here, we'd pretend it was snow," she said.

Rupert scooped up a handful of petals. He
threw them at Chloe. They fluttered in the
wind. They stuck in her hair.

Chloe gave Rupert a glare. "Go away," she
said.

And he did.

Chloe kicked at the petals. She frowned at
the ground. With Angel gone, there was
nothing to do.

36

Maybe I'll pretend Angel is invisible, thought Chloe. Maybe I'll pretend I made her disappear.

"*Alakabam-Kazoo!* You can come back now, Angel," said Chloe.

Angel did not come back.

"It takes more than magic to make a friend appear," said Chloe. She sighed. It wasn't much fun pretending alone.

Maybe I will make *myself* disappear, thought Chloe. I'll hide myself in a cherry tree. I'll hide myself from Rupert, and he will think I am invisible.

Chloe climbed the big cherry tree.

There in the branches was Rupert Raguso, hanging upside down from his knees.

Rupert ignored Chloe.

Chloe ignored Rupert.

They looked out at the empty street.

Chloe patted Angel's postcard. She wondered if Angel was swimming in the ocean. She wondered if Angel was playing in the sand. She wondered if Rupert knew what he was doing.

"Rupert," asked Chloe, "why are you hanging upside down?"

"I'm a monkey," said Rupert.

Chloe blinked. "You're pretending?"

Rupert didn't answer.

Chloe leaned way back. She hung by her knees and let go with her hands.

Rupert began to swing back and forth.

Chloe began to swing back and forth. "This is fun," she said. "From upside down, everything looks different."

Rupert smiled a shy smile.

Chloe made a monkey sound. "Ooo-ooo," she said.

"Ooo-ooo," said Rupert.

Chloe stared. "Even *you* look different from upside down."

"Different?" asked Rupert.

"Better," said Chloe.

"We are monkeys," she sang. "You are a monkey. I am a monkey. When Angel comes home, she can be a monkey, too."

Rupert-the-Monkey-Raguso began to blush.
"You are red as a cherry," said Chloe.
"But I feel like a banana," said Rupert.
Chloe laughed.
Rupert laughed.
"Ooo-ooo," they said together.

Rupert has changed, thought Chloe. It's almost like magic. "Let's send Angel a postcard," she said.

"A postcard of monkeys," said Rupert Raguso. "What should we say?"

"*I* know." Chloe pretended to write in the air:

Dear Angel,
Alakabam-Kazoo! We have a new friend on Sycamore Street.